YOUR FRIEND, PARKER

by **Parker Curry & Jessica Curry**
illustrated by **Brittany Jackson & Tajaé Keith**

Ready-to-Read

Simon Spotlight

New York   London   Toronto   Sydney   New Delhi

For my bestie, Gia, and all my friends and classmates at the Washington Yu Ying School
—P. C.

For my first friend, RGMEC
—J. C.

SIMON SPOTLIGHT

An imprint of Simon & Schuster Children's Publishing Division
1230 Avenue of the Americas, New York, New York 10020
This Simon Spotlight edition January 2022
Text copyright © 2022 by Parker Curry and Jessica Curry
Cover illustrations copyright © 2021, 2022 by Brittany Jackson
Interior illustrations copyright © 2022 by Brittany Jackson
Manufactured in the United States of America 1221 LAK
2 4 6 8 10 9 7 5 3 1
Library of Congress Cataloging-in-Publication Data
Names: Curry, Parker, author. | Curry, Jessica, author. | Jackson, Bea, 1986- illustrator. | Keith,
Tajaé, illustrator.
Title: Your friend, Parker / by Parker Curry & Jessica Curry ; cover illustrations by Brittany
Jackson ; interior illustrations by Tajaé Keith.
Description: New York : Simon Spotlight, an imprint of Simon & Schuster Children's
Publishing Division, 2022. | Summary: "Parker writes letters to her friend Gia while she travels
across the U.S. and visits states such as Georgia and New Mexico"—Provided by publisher.
Identifiers: LCCN 2021019591 (print) | LCCN 2021019592 (ebook) | ISBN 9781665902588
(paperback) | ISBN 9781665902595 (hardcover) | ISBN 9781665902601 (ebook)
Subjects: CYAC: Friendship—Fiction. | Travel—Fiction. | Letters—Fiction. | Curry, Parker—
Childhood and youth—Fiction. | African Americans—Fiction. | LCGFT: Autobiographical
fiction. | Picture books.
Classification: LCC PZ7.1.C8665 Yo 2021 (print) | LCC PZ7.1.C8665 (ebook) | DDC [E]—dc23
LC record available at https://lccn.loc.gov/2021019591
LC ebook record available at https://lccn.loc.gov/2021019592

My name is Parker.
This is my friend Gia.

We like dancing, drawing,
and eating ice cream.

We do everything together!

Today my family is leaving for a road trip.

"Can Gia come too?"
I ask.
My mom shakes her head.

I wave goodbye to Gia.
I will miss her so much!

Then I have an idea.
I can write letters
to Gia during
my trip.

Dear Gia,
We are in North Carolina!

Today we went to the beach with Papi and Nana.

I built a sandcastle.
It was almost taller
than you and me!

Then we ate lobsters
for dinner.
Yum!

Dear Gia,
We are in Georgia!

Today we went to
an aquarium.

I saw many jellyfish
dancing together.
I named one Parker
and another one Gia.

Later,
we bought peaches
at the market.

I wish I could send
one to you.

Dear Gia,
Remember when
we went sledding?

Today I went sledding,
but not in the snow.

It was in a sand dune
in New Mexico!

My sled was
our favorite colors!

At night we went to
a lantern festival.

I drew a picture
on my lantern.

I put a secret message
on it too.
Do you want to know
what it said?

It said, "I wish for Gia and me to be best friends forever!"

Then I watched the lantern
float up to the sky.

You are a great friend.
Please write back soon!

Love, your friend,
Parker

A FRIENDSHIP OF TWO WRITERS

Just like Parker and Gia, **ZORA NEALE HURSTON** and **DOROTHY WEST** were two friends who enjoyed writing letters to each other.

Zora (1891–1960) and Dorothy (1907–1998) first became friends in New York City. They were both writers and members of the Harlem Renaissance (say: REH-nuh-sonts), a cultural movement that celebrated African American arts and politics.

In the 1920s, Zora traveled to gather stories about African American folklore in the South. During her trips, the two friends wrote postcards and letters to each other. They also sent gifts like books and pecans.

Zora and Dorothy were far apart, but they stayed friends by doing what they both loved: writing. They even lived together after Zora returned to New York City.

You can write a letter to a friend or family member too. Draw a picture or add stickers to make it fun. Make sure to sign your name at the bottom!